TM

SAM AND DELILAH

BOOKS IN THE 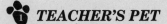 SERIES ™

SAM AND DELILAH

JENNY DALE

Illustrations by Mick Reid
Cover illustration by Michael Rowe

AN
**APPLE
PAPERBACK**

SCHOLASTIC INC.
New York Toronto London Auckland Sydney
Mexico City New Delhi Hong Kong

ISBN 0-439-21813-6

12 11 10 9 8   4 5 6/0

Printed in the U.S.A.   40
First Scholastic printing, May 2001

SPECIAL THANKS TO CHERITH BALDRY

CHAPTER ONE

Neil Parker carefully placed the last apple on top of the pyramid and squatted back on his heels to admire his work. Along with several of his classmates from Meadowbank School, he was helping to decorate Compton Parish Church, getting it ready for the harvest festival service. His apples glowed a warm red against the dark wood of the pulpit.

"Watch it!" he shouted as his friend Hasheem Lindon dumped a basket of green runner beans alongside the pyramid. "You'll knock it over."

"Sor-*ree!*" said Hasheem. "Hey, that's really good! Maybe you could get a job as a greengrocer when you leave school."

"No way!" Neil said. "I'm going to work with dogs."

Neil's family ran King Street Kennels, just outside

1

the country town of Compton. As far as Neil was concerned, nothing was more important to him than dogs. He couldn't imagine anything better than doing what his father did for a living. And he couldn't imagine anything *worse* than making apple pyramids!

Kathy Jones came staggering up under the weight of an enormous pumpkin. "What should I do with this?"

"Drop it on Smiler," Hasheem suggested.

Their class teacher, Mr. Hamley, was often known as Smiler — because he didn't. He was sitting in the front pew, scribbling on a seating plan. Kathy pretended she was going to throw the pumpkin at him.

"Don't blame Hasheem if we all get detention!" Neil said quickly. "Put it over there. It'll finish this section nicely."

Kathy lowered her pumpkin onto the stone floor of the church and stood up, panting. "Have you heard about the ghost?" she asked. Kathy was always first with any interesting gossip.

"Ghost? What ghost?" Neil looked at her suspiciously.

Before Kathy could reply, Hasheem raised his arms and waved them at her, making ghostly wailing noises.

"Could we have some quiet down there?" a voice rapped out.

Hasheem stopped being a ghost and turned

around. Mrs. Rowntree, the teacher in charge of the school choir, was giving him a severe look. Teachers didn't always see the funny side of Hasheem's jokes. "Uh . . . sorry, Mrs. Rowntree," he said.

"I should think so." Mrs. Rowntree turned back to her singers, who were facing her in the choir stalls. Emily, Neil's younger sister, was among them. She gave Neil a swift grin before turning back to watch Mrs. Rowntree, who was looking at her rather strictly. "From the beginning," Mrs. Rowntree said.

While the choir was going through the hymn for the umpteenth time, Neil, Kathy, and Hasheem sat on the stone steps below the church pulpit and whispered to each other quietly in order not to attract attention.

"My cousin Derek told me about it," Kathy said. "One of his friends saw it when he was taking a shortcut through the churchyard after dark."

"What did it do?" Hasheem asked, looking impressed.

"I don't know. Derek's friend didn't wait to find out."

Neil looked around the church. He didn't believe in ghosts, but he had to admit the church did have a spooky feel about it. The whole building was pitch-dark except the end where they were working, where the vicar had left the lights on. The high ceilings gave everything a strange, echoey sound. In front of them, gray pillars stretched up into the shadows of the roof.

"Have you noticed," asked Neil, "nobody ever sees a ghost? They always know somebody else who says they've seen one, but they never see one themselves."

"Derek's friend definitely saw this one," Kathy said, sounding injured.

Hasheem chuckled. "Wait till some guy in a white sheet chases you around the church, Neil!"

"Oh, it's not the ghost of a person," Kathy said. "It's a ghost dog!"

Neil stared at her with his mouth open. Before he could ask more about it, the choir finished their hymn and Mrs. Rowntree dismissed them. They came milling out of the choir stalls and down the steps. Emily came over to Neil.

"What do you mean, a ghost dog?" Neil was still trying to talk to Kathy, but she jumped up and went to join her sister.

"It's true," Emily said. "Julie told me."

"Did Julie see it?"

"No. But she knows somebody in the church choir who did. She saw it when she was going home after practice last week."

Neil shrugged. "Typical!" he said.

Gossip was buzzing all around them. From the few scraps that he could hear, Neil realized that everybody was talking about the ghost dog.

"It's a big, black dog," Emily went on. "And do you know what Julie's grandmother told her?" She clutched at Neil's arm and lowered her voice. "She says that if you see the ghost of a black dog, it means someone is going to die!" Emily gazed at Neil wide-eyed, her face pale against untidy dark hair.

"That's ridiculous!" Neil said confidently. "People die because they get old, or sick, or have an accident. Not because some ghost dog tells them to!"

"Don't you think it's even a little bit spooky?"

"No, I —" Neil broke off, and the rest of the voices faded away quickly as Mr. Hamley got up from the front pew.

"OK," Mr. Hamley said. "Attention, please. The decorators have done a marvelous job arranging nature's wondrous bounty, and the choir sounded like angels." Somebody giggled, and Mr. Hamley smiled. "You can all go home in a minute, but first there's something I want to say. I've heard several people talking about rumors of a ghost dog here in the churchyard." His smile faded.

Uh-oh, Neil thought. Here we go.

Mr. Hamley went on, "I'm surprised that sensible young people like yourselves can believe such nonsense." His face and his voice hardened; he was beginning to sound angry. "Once a rumor like this takes hold, there's no stopping it. You might get a thrill out of it, but younger children, especially in the lower grades, could get seriously upset. So I want it to stop here and now." His eyes raked across Neil and his friends. He spoke slowly and forcefully.

"There are no such things as ghosts. And I don't want to hear any more about this. Is that clear?"

A chorus of voices said, "Yes, sir!"

Neil wasn't sure that they all meant it.

It was growing dark by the time Neil and Emily left the church. They had to walk down a long and winding path through the churchyard to where they had left their bikes. Some of their friends' parents had come to pick them up, and there were too many people around, too much noise and light from cars entering and leaving the parking lot, just off the road, for a ghost to make its appearance.

Once they were well away from Mr. Hamley's ears, Emily said, "Neil — you really don't think there's a ghost, do you?"

"Of course not. Just the same," he added, as they reached their bikes and he fished in his pocket for the key to his lock, "let's not say anything to Squirt."

Squirt, Neil's five-year-old sister Sarah, was sitting at the kitchen table when he and Emily arrived home. She was wearing her pajamas and she was in a terrible mood. "Why can't I go?" she moaned.

"Because it's too late for you," said their mother, Carole Parker. "It's nearly your bedtime."

"Don't worry, Sarah," Kate McGuire said. "You can stay up a bit later tonight. Why don't you draw me a picture?"

Kate, the Parkers' kennel assistant, was a tall girl with long, blond hair. She enjoyed working with dogs and she was always cheerful. Bob Parker, Neil's father, often said he didn't know what he would do without Kate.

"What's all this about staying up late?" asked Emily.

Kate grinned and winked at her. "When I'm baby-sitting, what I say goes!"

Sarah jumped up to get paper and crayons.

Carole swung around to see Neil and Emily in the doorway. "Thank goodness you're back! Your harvest festival rehearsal *would* have to be tonight. Go straight upstairs and get changed, or we'll be late."

For a minute, Neil hardly recognized his mother. She looked taller than ever and incredibly elegant in a plain, black dress and long silver earrings. For the first time in ages the whole family was invited to a party that night. "Mom!" he said. "Do I have to go? I haven't walked Sam yet."

Sam, Neil's black-and-white Border collie, was resting in his basket, and cocked an ear at the mention of his name. Sam lifted his glossy head as Neil approached and nuzzled his hand affectionately. He looked so different now from the helpless puppy who had been found abandoned by the train tracks four years ago. The Parkers had just opened the rescue center where they looked after stray dogs. Sam was one of their first customers, and they'd decided to keep him. Now his coat and eyes shone with health. Sam was ready for anything.

"Kate walked him," said Carole. "And there isn't any time to be difficult. Go and wash up — and put your new shirt on. And do something about your hair! It looks as if it doesn't know what a comb is."

Neil knew when there was no point in arguing. He turned and went upstairs.

"Consider yourself lucky," muttered Emily, as she followed him. "I've got to wear a dress!"

Neil changed into the new shirt. It had blue and yellow stripes, and Neil liked it, but he wasn't going to admit that to his mom. He did his best with his unruly brown hair, trying to slick it down with a wet comb, but two spiky clumps on top insisted on sticking right up. Hoping his mother wouldn't notice, he went downstairs again.

Emily was already there, wriggling uncomfortably in a red dress. Bob Parker had also appeared. He was a large man and, in a suit and tie, was looking just as uncomfortable as Neil felt.

"Bob," said Carole, sounding disappointed, "you forgot to shave."

Bob rubbed a hand across his chin. "No, I didn't. I'm growing a beard."

Carole slapped her forehead. Her silver earrings shivered. "Give me strength!" she said. "The one time we have to dress up, and you decide to grow a beard!"

Neil grinned. "It's all the rage, Mom. Designer stubble."

Carole glanced at her watch; Neil thought she was trying not to laugh. "Well, it's too late now. We have to go."

Waving good-bye to Kate and Sarah and Sam, they set off in their green Range Rover with the King Street Kennels logo emblazoned on the side.

Neil usually didn't enjoy grown-ups' parties, but he had to admit he was curious about this one. They were on their way to Old Mill Farm, which had recently been taken over by new owners. Mike Turner, the local vet, had introduced Neil's dad to Richard Hammond when they were both at his Compton office. Richard had invited the Parkers to the housewarming party, where the rest of the family would meet their new neighbors for the first time.

The King Street Kennels exercise field bordered part of the Hammonds' land, but the farmhouse was some distance away by road, mostly along a winding lane. At last, this gave way to a wide, graveled space in front of the farmhouse. It was a converted watermill, and the old wheel still stood beside the house where the stream gurgled along.

Richard Hammond, a tall, fair-haired young man, greeted the Parkers at the door and showed them into a large room with a polished wooden floor and long velvet curtains. Small groups of people were already standing there, and a hum of talk and laughter filled the room.

"Wow!" Neil murmured. "This is a farmhouse?"

Richard served the Parkers drinks from a table covered with a white cloth. Emily saw someone from her class at school and went off to join her. Neil stood holding his orange juice. He was ready to be bored, but he felt better when he saw some people he knew: Mike Turner and the local doctor, Alex Harvey. He felt better still when he saw a dog.

It was a black-and-white Border collie, just like Sam, though Neil guessed this dog was younger. It sat on a rug in front of the fireplace, head up, eyes bright and alert. Light gleamed on its glossy black-and-white coat.

Neil wriggled his way past a group of guests and squatted down beside the dog. He reached out a hand for the dog to sniff and then scratched it gently behind the ears.

"Hello," he said. "What's your name?"

"She's named Delilah."

At the sound of her name, the dog thumped her tail gently against the floor. Neil looked up. Standing over him was a young woman, small and thin with black hair in short, tousled curls.

"Hello," she said. "I'm Jane Hammond." She sat on the rug beside Delilah and rumpled the collie's ears.

"She's great," said Neil.

"Yes, she knows it, too. Don't you, Delilah?" She smiled at Neil. "Do you like dogs?"

Neil thought it would take a year to answer that accurately. "You could say that! I'm Neil Parker," he said. "I live at King Street Kennels."

Jane laughed. "Then of course you like dogs!"

"I love dogs," Neil confessed. "And I've got a Border collie just like this one. His name's Sam."

Jane's eyes twinkled. "That wouldn't be short for Samson, would it?"

Neil stared at her for a minute until he grasped

what she meant. "Hey, Sam and Delilah!" he exclaimed. "That's cool!"

He started to tell Jane about how he came to own Sam, and then about training him and how well Sam did in Agility Competitions at local country shows.

"Delilah does Agility, too," said Jane. "Maybe we'll meet in the ring." Then she added, "I think I might have seen your Sam. At least, there's been another Border collie paying us the occasional visit since we moved in."

"That would be Sam," said Neil. "Our land joins yours. Though he doesn't usually wander this far."

"Yes, well, it might be better —" Jane started to say, when Richard Hammond interrupted.

"When do you want to eat?" he asked his wife.

"Soon." Jane scrambled to her feet. "Nice to meet you, Neil."

"Yes, it's great to meet you, too," Neil said enthusiastically. "You know, the last man who owned this place, Philip Kendall, couldn't stand dogs. He wasn't even a real farmer — he wanted to pull all this down and build a supermarket. I'm really glad he's gone."

Jane's expression, which had been friendly, suddenly turned cold. "Really?" she said. "Then I think you've already met my father."

CHAPTER TWO

"Well, how was I to know?" Neil complained. "Nobody told me. And I said I was sorry."

Bob Parker was driving the Range Rover back along the lane toward the kennel. "I wouldn't worry," he said. "I don't think Jane was too upset."

"She's really nice," Emily said. "I don't see how she could be related to that horrible Philip Kendall."

"Richard explained it to me while we were having dinner," Carole said. "He's just finished his studies at Padsham Agricultural College, but he didn't have any land of his own. When he married Jane, her father gave them Old Mill Farm as a wedding present."

"It was a pretty good present," Neil said. "Maybe Philip Kendall isn't so bad after all."

Bob laughed. "He's probably OK if he's your *father*."

Emily, who had never liked Kendall, gave a disapproving sniff, and yawned. "It was a good party."

"And they have a fantastic dog!" Neil was enthusiastic again, forgetting his embarrassment. "Jane says Delilah does Agility competitions, too. I wonder if Sam and Delilah could train together?"

The harvest festival took place after school on Thursday. To Neil, it seemed to last forever. He might have enjoyed it under different circumstances, but he was too worried about the time he was missing with Sam. Neil was training him for an Agility competition in Padsham on the following Saturday. He had missed one evening's training session already because of the rehearsal for the harvest festival, and now he was missing another because of the service itself.

By the time the vicar had said the final prayer and everyone started to file out of the church, it was starting to get dark. The church was bathed in a spooky low light.

"Do you think we'll see the ghost?" Emily whispered, as they walked down the path.

"Ghosts don't exist," Neil said dismissively. "And you'll be in big trouble if Smiler hears you say they do."

The following day was Neil's last chance to get Sam into top form for the competition, and he was determined to make the most of it. As soon as the bell rang for the end of school he dashed for his bike and rode home. Abandoning the bike by the side gate, he hurried into the courtyard between the two kennel blocks and whistled for Sam.

Sam didn't appear. Calling his name, Neil went on into the garden, expecting to find him in his favorite spot under the hedge. He called several times, looking under the bushes and over the fence into the exercise field. Still no sign of Sam.

Annoyed at the time he was wasting, Neil went into the house. The kitchen was empty but he heard faint sounds from the office and went in to find his mother at the computer.

"Where's Sam?" he asked.

Carole looked up from her typing. "Isn't he in the garden?"

"No."

"Then maybe he's gone to visit his lady friend at Old Mill Farm. Don't worry, Neil. Sam knows where he lives."

"But I need him for training," Neil said.

He went outside again and had another look around the front of the house. There was still no sign of Sam, but the Range Rover was just turning into the driveway. Bob Parker had brought Emily and Sarah home from school.

"What's the problem?" Bob asked.

"Sam's disappeared. Mom thinks he's gone to Old Mill Farm."

Emily giggled. "He's got a girlfriend!"

"But the competition's tomorrow," Neil said. "He needs to train."

"I know," Emily said, serious again. "Let's go and set the course up in the field. Maybe he'll be back by the time it's ready."

"And if not," Bob added, "I'll give Jane a call. If he's up at Old Mill Farm I could go and get him."

Feeling slightly better, Neil led the way to the storeroom between the two kennel blocks. Here he kept the homemade obstacles for Sam's Agility training: the barrel, a set of steps, the tunnel, tires, and planks and bricks for the walkway and seesaw. Emily helped him haul out the various items and they began to set up the course in the field.

Neil kept calling Sam, but the Border collie did not appear until the course was almost ready. Just as Neil was thinking that he would have to ask his dad to phone Mrs. Hammond, he saw Sam bounding across the exercise field from the direction of the hedge that divided King Street from Old Mill Farm.

Relieved, Neil called, "Sam! Here, boy!"

Sam came up and flopped to the ground beside him, tongue lolling out as he panted, eyes bright. Neil patted him. "Had a nice time?" he asked. "I hope you've got some energy left!"

Sam had the chance for a rest while Neil and Emily finished building the seesaw from planks and bricks. This was the part of the course that Sam liked least, and Neil always gave him plenty of practice with it. Once it was ready, Neil hauled the steps into place — the last obstacle — and Emily went to stand by an imaginary finish line.

"I'll time him," she called to Neil. "Ready when you are."

Neil raised a hand to her. "OK, Sam," he said. "Up you go."

The Border collie gave him a look and then got to his feet and loped after Neil to the start of the course. Neil bent down to hold his collar while he waited for Emily to give the signal.

"Right, Sam! *Go!*"

Sam hopped over the first jump, slithered along the tunnel, but seemed to hesitate in front of the hanging tire. "Come on, Sam," Neil encouraged him. "You can do it!" He knew every second would count in the competition the following afternoon.

Sam jumped for the tire, scrabbled to push himself through it, and was off again, through the barrel and weaving between the upright poles. Neil pounded alongside. Then it was the seesaw. Sam ran up to the center, hesitated while the seesaw tilted, and ran easily down the other side. Up the steps. Down. And the last race for the finish.

When he reached Emily, Sam lay down again, panting, while Neil patted him and rumpled his

ears. "Good Boy — well done!" He looked up at Emily. "Well?"

Emily was frowning as she studied her watch. "Fifty-eight seconds," she said. "That's about five seconds slower than his average time over this course."

Neil gazed down at Sam. "He misjudged that tire," he said, more to himself than Emily.

"Well, the space looks awfully small. I know if I were a dog I'd be afraid of getting stuck."

"And he's tired," Neil agreed. "He's probably been playing with Delilah all afternoon. And he hasn't trained since Tuesday — I knew I should have had more time to work with him!"

"Do you want to try him again?" Emily asked.

"No. He'll just be more tired. I'm going to see that he gets a good rest before the competition tomorrow.

Anyway," Neil added, as he started dismantling the course, "speed isn't everything."

Whenever Neil walked over a real Agility course, he felt nervous. Everything was bigger and brighter than the homemade course in the field, so that it looked more difficult. Luckily, Neil thought as he studied the course at the Padsham show next day, the difference didn't seem to bother Sam.

Instead of planks and bricks, the jumps were gates with shrubs and flowers at each side. The seesaw and the dogwalk were brightly colored. The yellow contact points that the dogs had to touch as they went around the course were everywhere. Neil was always terrified that Sam would get so enthusiastic that he would miss some of the contact points and have to take a penalty.

"Hi there. Looks fierce, doesn't it?" a voice said from behind him.

Neil turned. Jane Hammond was standing there, smiling as if she'd forgotten all the rude things he'd said about her father.

"Hello," he said. "Is Delilah competing?"

Jane nodded. "She loves it."

"So does Sam. Dad says Border collies are good at Agility because they're fast and clever and they have good memory."

"That's Delilah, all right!" Jane agreed. "But listen, Neil, there's something I wanted to say to you.

Sam was up at the farm again yesterday, and I don't think it's a good idea to let him wander, because —"

"Oh, I know," Neil interrupted, grinning. "He didn't do such a good practice because he was tired."

"Yes, but —"

Jane never finished. Just then the course manager came up to give the competitors their instructions. And by the time Neil had taken in everything he needed to know, he had forgotten that Jane was trying to tell him something.

Neil took Sam from his parents, and when his class was called he went to stand near the entrance to the ring. Bob and Carole were standing by the sideline with Emily and Sarah, ready to cheer him on. Sarah gave him an encouraging wave.

Jane Hammond was waiting nearby with Delilah. Neil noticed for the first time how proper Mrs. Hammond looked in corduroy jeans, a blue shirt, and polished boots. Delilah looked good, too, her coat brushed so that it shone, tail waving with enthusiasm. Neil was ready to bet that Sam's new friend was very good indeed. He grinned and pulled Sam back as the Border collie tugged on his leash toward her, wanting to say hello.

The first dog to go was a golden Labrador. He managed a clear round, but Neil guessed he wasn't fast enough. Next was a German shepherd, which was too fast and missed several contact points.

Then the announcer's voice came through the

loudspeakers: "Next we have Jane Hammond and Lakeview Delilah!"

The crowd applauded as Jane led Delilah into the ring. The Border collie made eagerly for the starting point, and Jane stooped to calm her down. Then the whistle went, and Delilah was off.

Over the first jump and up onto the dogwalk. Jane was beside her, urging her on, but Delilah didn't seem to need it. She made it look so smooth and easy. Through the barrel. Another jump. Through the hanging tire, where Sam had hesitated in practice. Weaving in and out of the poles. Delilah disappeared into the long tunnel and appeared again at the other end faster than Neil thought possible.

The crowd erupted in applause as Delilah gracefully tackled the seesaw and then streaked toward the finish. Neil found himself already swallowing disappointment, even while he was thrilled at the sight of a dog and owner working together so brilliantly. "Well, Sam," he laughed. "Follow that!"

Soon it was Sam's turn. As Neil led him out, he concentrated on what they had to do. He was aware of the crowd's applause, but he could not pay any attention to it.

The whistle sounded. Sam set off. As soon as he started to move, Neil thought he could see a difference. Sam usually enjoyed himself so much that he sometimes made mistakes. Now it was as if he were thinking hard. He touched the first contact point,

then the next. And the one after that. He was heading for the tire. "Come on, boy!" Neil called, almost
afraid to watch. But Sam was up and through. He
nipped neatly in and out of the poles, nosed his way
into the tunnel, and bounded up the slope of the seesaw. As it tilted, his paws scrabbled. "Steady, boy!"
Neil said. Sam kept his balance, half-slid down the
other side, and touched the contact point. Then he
headed for the finish.

Neil paced him and knelt beside him at the end of
the course, hugging him. He could feel Sam's heart
pounding and hear his panting breath. "That was
great, Sam!" he said. It had been a perfect round. All
Neil asked himself was, had Sam been fast enough
to beat Delilah?

Bob and Carole Parker forged their way through
the crowds to meet him, with Emily and Sarah in
tow. Bob bent down and made a fuss of their proud,
beaming collie.

"Well done, Neil," his dad congratulated him.

"Sam, too," Neil said.

"Yes, Sam too. I don't think I've ever seen him run
better."

They watched the last few dogs in the class. One of
them, an Airedale terrier, was very good too, but Neil
still didn't think there was a dog there who could
beat Delilah. He saw Richard and Jane Hammond,
watching not far away, looking happy and excited.

And no wonder, Neil thought. There couldn't be much doubt about who had won.

It seemed like hours before the loudspeaker crackled into life with the results of the Agility class. "First — Lakeview Delilah!" Of course, Neil thought, as he joined in the applause. He glanced down at Sam, sitting at his feet. "Your girlfriend won, Sam," he said. "Are you —"

"Second . . ." the announcer said, "Neilsboy Puppy Patrol Sam!"

Emily tugged Neil's arm. "Neil, did you hear? Sam was second!"

Neil blinked at her. "Yes, of course I heard!" He squatted down beside Sam and hugged him again. "Sam, that was just great. You're going to be a real champion!"

He was still crouched beside Sam when a pair of polished boots came into view and Jane Hammond said, "Congratulations."

Neil looked up. "You too," he said. "Delilah was fantastic! Better watch out for us next time, though!"

Sam got up and padded a few steps to where Delilah was sitting at Jane's feet. The two dogs nuzzled each other affectionately. Neil laughed, but to his surprise, he saw that Jane was looking annoyed.

"We'd better be going," she said. "Come on, Delilah."

Neil got to his feet and stared after her as she

turned and walked away with Delilah at heel. Sam
started to follow, and then came back to Neil; Neil
thought he looked just as bewildered as he felt himself.

"What on earth's got into her?" he asked.

CHAPTER THREE

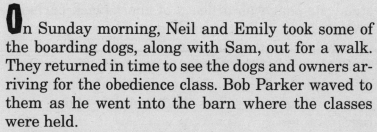

On Sunday morning, Neil and Emily took some of
the boarding dogs, along with Sam, out for a walk.
They returned in time to see the dogs and owners ar-
riving for the obedience class. Bob Parker waved to
them as he went into the barn where the classes
were held.

The barn was new, rebuilt after the old one had
been destroyed in a fire. A sign over its door said
RED'S BARN, in honor of the beautiful Irish setter who
had saved Neil from the fire and died of his injuries.
Neil liked to think that his friend Red would always
be remembered at King Street.

Neil and Emily returned the dogs to their pens. As
they were crossing the courtyard again, they saw a

woman coming through the gate that led to the front of the house. She had a small black dog in her arms.

"Hello," Neil said. "Have you come for the obedience class? They're just starting — they're in the barn."

"Obedience class?" The woman looked as if she didn't know what he was talking about. "No, this isn't my dog. She was sitting on my step this morning. You do take stray dogs here, don't you?"

"Yes, that's right."

Emily stroked the little dog's head as it snuggled up in the woman's arm. It was a miniature poodle, but it hadn't been given the usual poodle clip. Instead, its coat was a fleece of short black curls all over its body. It looked around at its new surroundings, bright-eyed with interest.

"She's lovely," Emily said admiringly. "Look, she's got a collar, and a tag." She examined the tag and added, "Her name's Tess. And there's a phone number."

"Well then . . ." said Neil.

"It's not as easy as that," the woman said. "I called the number myself, and the man who answered told me he'd just moved in. It's a rented apartment and he never met the person who had it before him. Tess isn't his." She scratched the dog's ears gently. "Poor little thing."

Neil suddenly felt hot with anger. "You mean somebody moved away and left their dog behind?"

"She's very thin," the woman said. "I can feel all her ribs. I fed her, and she wolfed it down as if she hadn't seen food for a month."

"Well, you've brought her to the right place," said Neil. "We'll go and find my mom, and she can take your name and address."

"And I'll settle Tess into a pen in the rescue center," said Emily. She took the little dog and cuddled her. Tess licked her face.

Neil showed the woman into the office, where Carole made a note of her name and address and promised to let her know what happened.

That night, Neil was lying in bed, drowsily planning Sam's Agility training. Suddenly, a scream ripped

through the quiet house. Wide-awake, Neil sat bolt upright.

When he heard the scream again, he realized it was coming from the direction of Sarah's bedroom. He got out of bed and padded into the passage in time to see his mom appear at the head of the stairs. She opened Sarah's door and went in. Neil followed.

Sarah was sitting up in bed, screaming. Neil realized she was still asleep and in the middle of a nightmare. Carole sat on the bed beside her, put an arm around her shoulders, and gave her a gentle shake.

"Sarah . . . shhh, love. Wake up. It's all right."

Bob appeared in the doorway, with Emily just behind him, yawning and rubbing sleep out of her eyes. "What's going on?" she asked.

Sarah's screaming had given way to noisy sobbing. She was clinging to her mother.

"It's the big, black dog!" she wailed. "It's under my bed!"

Carole looked puzzled. "What big, black dog?" she asked. "What's she talking about?"

"Oh, it's just some stupid story at school," Neil said. "People are saying there's the ghost of a black dog haunting the churchyard."

"It means someone's going to die!" Sarah sobbed. "And it's under my bed!"

Neil got down on his hands and knees. "There's nothing under your bed, Squirt," he said. "At least . . ." Groping around, he pulled out a book, a T-shirt and one sneaker. "Just these. No big, black dog. Honest."

Sarah's sobs sank to quieter hiccuping. She gave Neil a doubtful look, as if she weren't quite ready to believe that he was telling the truth.

"You've had a nightmare," Bob said. "You know there aren't any ghosts, except in stories. And dogs are nice animals. They won't hurt you."

Sarah sniffed. "I thought it meant Fudge was going to die."

Sarah's hamster, Fudge, was rattling around inside the wheel in his cage oblivious to all the noise and fuss. Everyone could see that he was very much alive. After watching him for a minute, Sarah was ready to believe it, too.

"You haven't been telling her these silly stories, have you?" Carole asked Neil and Emily.

"We wouldn't!" Emily said indignantly.

"It's all over school," Neil explained.

"I suppose it's somebody's idea of a joke," Carole said. "If you hear any more of this nonsense, I hope you'll put a stop to it." She wiped Sarah's tears away with a tissue. "Now, back to bed, both of you. Sarah, you settle down, and I'll read you another story."

Neil and Emily paused at the door to Neil's bedroom.

"Put a stop to it," Emily said, stifling another yawn. "I wish we could."

"Well," Neil said thoughtfully, "we'll never stop

people gossiping, whatever Mr. Hamley says. The only thing we *could* do is find out the truth about this so-called ghost."

Though Neil and Emily discussed what they might do about the ghost dog the next morning, they didn't come up with any ideas. No one at school seemed to know where the story had started. Nobody admitted to seeing the ghost, though plenty of people knew someone who had. Neil didn't like to ask too many questions in case Mr. Hamley heard him. He was getting himself onto Smiler's bad list often enough already, without the ghost dog making it worse.

He had no time to hang around and talk to people after school. Now that it was getting dark earlier, it was hard to give Sam his regular exercise. Neil started to hurry home as fast as he could to take the Border collie for a run on the ridgeway beyond the exercise field.

One evening they climbed to the very top of the hill. Neil strolled along the ridgeway track, watching the sun go down over Compton. The nearby trees were casting long shadows. Sam had disappeared into the bushes somewhere, pretending to chase rabbits.

Then the silence was broken by a flurry of excited barking. Neil whistled, and not one but two Border collies came dashing out of the trees, jumping and circling around each other. Neil laughed. "Hi there, Delilah!"

He stood and watched the two dogs running and playing, and only gradually became aware of a voice shouting something from further along the ridge-way. A minute later, Jane Hammond appeared, almost running, her face red and looking annoyed.

"Delilah — here, Delilah! Heel!"

Delilah, obviously not as well-trained as Sam, took no notice. Jane strode up to Neil. Neil started to say hello, but Jane was not listening to him.

"Neil Parker, can't you keep that dog of yours on a leash?"

"Why?" Neil asked. He felt completely confused. "He's not doing any harm — they're only having fun."

"Fun!" Jane looked really annoyed and, for some reason, ready to lose her temper. "Look, Neil, I just don't want Sam getting together with Delilah. Can't you do something about it?"

"I still don't see why," Neil said. "They like each other."

"They like each other too much. Delilah! Heel!"

Jane slapped the leash she carried against her boot, but Delilah was still feeling playful. Neil called to Sam, who came at once and sat panting on the grass by Neil's side. Delilah nosed after him, and then at last went over to Jane.

"Bad dog!" Jane said, as she clipped on the leash. Neil thought she looked even angrier, perhaps because Sam had obeyed right away when her own dog hadn't. "Neil," she went on, "can we get this straight once and for all. I don't want Sam coming over to the farm to see Delilah. Will you please keep him on your own property."

"Well . . ." Neil too was starting to feel annoyed. "It's not right to keep a dog tied up the whole time. And he knows how to open the latch on the garden gate . . ."

"Then get a new latch!" Jane said. "Just keep him away, OK?" She tugged at Delilah's leash, returning the way she had come, making the unwilling dog go with her. Neil stood with his mouth open as Jane turned back and added, "If I find Sam over at the farm again, I'll be calling your father."

CHAPTER FOUR

The sun had gone down, and it was rapidly growing darker as Neil reached King Street Kennels with Sam. He took the Border collie straight into the kitchen, where he found his father chopping onions for one of his famous spaghetti sauces. "Dad, I just met —" he began.

Bob interrupted him. "I just got a phone call from Mike Turner about Tess," he said.

"Yes?"

"You know Mike looked her over the other day? Well, he recognized her and looked her up in his records."

"He knows who owns her?" Neil asked eagerly.

"Yes. Somebody by the name of Ann Barton. She took Tess in to him just a few months ago for her injections. He has her address and phone number, but it's the same number as on Tess's tag."

"So you think this Ann Barton just went away and didn't bother to take her dog with her?" Neil said.

"It looks like it," Bob said, but he didn't sound certain. "Tess is such a nice little dog. She's been very well-trained and looked after, until very recently. I could easily find her a new home, but I think we should make a few more inquiries first. I might find out who owns the building and see if they know where Ann Barton has gone."

"I could put her information on the King Street Kennels website," Neil suggested. "We get quite a few hits on the rescue dogs section now. Somebody might recognize her."

"Yes. Do that."

Bob finished his onions and started looking around for the right pan. Neil sat down at the kitchen table and told him about meeting Jane Hammond on the ridgeway. "I can't see what she was getting so worked up about," he finished.

"Ah, well." Bob rubbed his chin. Neil noticed that his beard was coming along well; he looked like a real villain. "I expect Jane doesn't want Delilah to have Sam's pups," he said.

"Oh," Neil said. "But why not? That'd be really great."

Bob stopped what he was doing, leaned against the counter, and folded his arms. "The trouble is,

Neil, that Delilah's a pedigree dog and Sam isn't. So if Delilah has Sam's pups, they won't be pedigree either."

"Sam *might* be a pedigree," Neil said, defending his beloved dog. "He just hasn't got the papers to prove it."

"That's the problem," Bob said. "Those papers are important. Without them, he can't be registered with the Kennel Club, and his pups can't be registered either."

"But he *is* registered," Neil said. "I filled his form in."

"Yes, but that was only the Obedience and Working Trials register, so that he can take part in Agility competitions. He's not eligible for the breed register, because he hasn't got his original papers. You couldn't show him, and Jane couldn't show his pups. And if she wanted to sell them she wouldn't get such a good price."

"Oh." Neil digested that. "Well, then, maybe we can trace Sam's original owner and find out about his pedigree."

"Come on, Neil," his father said. "After all this time? Whoever left Sam to wander by the railroad tracks didn't care what happened to him and won't want to be traced."

"I suppose not." Neil let out a massive sigh. "I still don't see why Sam and Delilah can't be friends."

Bob grinned. "With a male and female dog, sooner

or later it'll go beyond being friends. If Sam goes up there when Delilah's in heat, she could easily end up pregnant. I expect Jane wants to mate Delilah with a pedigree dog."

"Huh!" Neil reached down and patted Sam, who was sitting by his chair. "It's not fair. You're just as good as any pedigree dog, aren't you, boy? Better."

"I can see Jane's point," said Bob. "We want to be good neighbors. I agree with you, Neil, we can't keep Sam shut in all day, or expect him to go everywhere on a leash. But we might try a bit harder to keep him away from the farm. For a start, I'll do something about the latch on the gate to the field."

"All right." Neil didn't feel too happy, though. He knew how proud Sam was of being able to jump up and lift the latch with his nose. It seemed a pity that he wouldn't have the chance to show off anymore.

"By the way, Neil," his dad said, turning back to the stove, "there's a big Agility contest coming up in Manchester next month. I've got the forms from the contest manager. I suppose you'll want to enter Sam?"

"'Course I do." Neil couldn't help admitting to himself that he would get a lot of satisfaction out of competing against Jane Hammond again and showing her what a terrific dog Sam was. "This time we'll really give Delilah a run for her money!"

The next day Bob fixed a bolt on the gate, and for nearly a week there were no more expeditions to Old

Mill Farm. Sam seemed restless, though, and Neil thought it wouldn't be long before he managed to force his way through the hedge. When he walked Sam on the ridgeway after school, he didn't see Jane and Delilah again, and he guessed that Jane must be walking Delilah at a different time.

Just before winter vacation, Neil hurried home from school as usual to give Sam his walk. As he was about to look for Sam in the garden, his mother appeared from the office. "Neil, I've just spoken to Jane Hammond on the phone," she said. "Sam's over at Old Mill Farm again."

"Uh-oh," said Neil. "He must have made a hole in the hedge."

"I can't get him because your dad's got the car. Jane says she's in the middle of something right now but she'll bring him over in an hour or so. She didn't sound pleased."

"It's a lot of fuss about nothing," Neil said. "Sam's a smashing dog, pedigree or no pedigree." He saw that Carole was looking impatient and added quickly, "OK, Mom, stay calm. I'll watch out for her."

"Call me when she comes," Carole said, and she vanished into the office again.

Neil tried to do some homework while he waited for Jane Hammond to bring Sam back, but he couldn't concentrate very well. After less than half an hour, he strolled over to the front of the house to wait in the fading light. Twenty minutes later Jane drove through the gateway in her large, brown Volkswagen. Neil tapped on the office window, signaled to his mom, and went to meet Jane as she jumped out of the car. She was talking even before Neil had a chance to greet her.

"Neil, I've just about had enough of this."

Sam hopped out after her and went over to Neil, where he sat down. Neil rumpled his ears.

"I'm sorry," said Neil. "Sam doesn't understand, that's all."

"Then it's up to you to do something. Can't you —"

"But Sam —"

"Hello, Jane." Carole's voice interrupted before the argument could get going. She gave Neil a look that said clearly, *Let me handle this*.

"Look, Carole," Jane said, "I just can't have Sam and Delilah getting together like this. Delilah's parents are both champions —"

"And Sam's a rescue dog," Carole finished for her. "I know. But what can we do about it?"

"We have tried to keep Sam at home," Neil pointed out.

"*Tried* isn't good enough," Jane snapped. "Surely you could do something about your garden fence?"

"Jane," Carole said, "can you imagine the time and money it would take for both of us to fix our fences so that two determined dogs couldn't get at each other?"

"It's not two determined dogs," Jane said angrily. "It's your dog coming where he's not wanted."

"Delilah wants him," Neil protested.

Jane looked down at Sam, who was sitting at Neil's feet, the picture of obedience. Some of her annoyance died away, and she sighed. "I know she does. I'm at my wits' end," she admitted.

"Honestly," said Carole, "I think the best thing you could do is mate Delilah as soon as possible. I'm sure Mike Turner could give you details of good stud dogs in the area. And then —"

She broke off as another car turned into the driveway. Neil didn't recognize it at first, until Emily scrambled out of the passenger seat. Then he saw that the driver was Mrs. Baker, Julie's mom. Emily had gone to play with her friend after school.

"Neil!" Emily gasped as she grabbed him. Her face was white and her dark hair was all over the place. "Neil, we've just seen the ghost dog!"

CHAPTER FIVE

"**W**hat?" Neil exclaimed.

"It's true!" Emily's friend Julie climbed out of the back of the car and her Old English sheepdog Ben followed after her. "It was big — bigger than Ben, even!"

"I'm sorry," Mrs. Baker said, walking around the car to talk to Carole. "I let them go up to the church-yard — I didn't think they'd come to any harm if they had Ben with them, but then they came back with this ghost story. Emily wanted to tell you all about it, so I brought her home."

"Thank you," said Carole. "Emily, are you all right?"

"Yes, Mom." Emily was starting to look calmer. "The dog didn't do anything. But it was scary. It —"

"Let's talk about it inside," Carole suggested. "We can discuss it over a cup of coffee."

"We won't stay, thanks," said Mrs. Baker. "I'm expecting Julie's dad home any minute. Come on, Julie."

Julie made a face, then heaved Ben back into the car and got herself in, waving to Emily. Neil and Emily led the way indoors, and to Neil's surprise, Jane accepted Carole's invitation for a drink and came in with them.

While Carole made coffee, Neil poured orange juice for himself and Emily and put a plate of cookies on the kitchen table. "What did you see, Em?"

Emily wrapped her hands around her glass. She seemed much happier now she was in the warm, bright kitchen.

"Julie and I went up to the churchyard to see if we could see the ghost," she explained. "You know, Neil, we said we'd try to find out more, but I haven't noticed you doing very much."

"I've been busy," said Neil, defensively.

"Anyway, we went up there today. The churchyard's massive — it goes a long way behind the church, and it's full of hundreds of old tombstones and graves. More than I'd ever imagined." She shuddered, as if she was enjoying the thrill. "It was really spooky. Anyway, we looked around and didn't see anything. Then just as we were going back to Julie's, we saw it."

Carole put a cup of coffee and the sugar bowl in front of Jane and brought her own coffee to the table. "What did you see?"

"A big, black shadow!" Emily pitched her voice low. "It was beside a tombstone, which was shaped like an angel with big wings. We didn't dare go past it."

"What did Ben do?" Neil asked.

"He just froze. His legs went all stiff, and his hair stood on end." Thinking of the shaggy Old English sheepdog, Neil thought that must have been a sight worth seeing. "And he growled. He sounded really fierce."

Neil found that almost as hard to believe in as the ghost. Ben was the gentlest dog on the whole planet.

"What happened then?" Jane asked. She looked interested and sympathetic, hardly the same person as the one who had been arguing furiously in the driveway.

"The ghost went away," Emily said. "It vanished, just like that!"

"It must have been a trick of the light," Carole said.

"No, it wasn't!"

"But honestly, Em, you can't expect us to believe you saw a ghost!" Neil said. "There are no such things."

"Well, I definitely saw something!" Emily insisted. She was starting to turn red with anger. "They say that if you see it somebody's going to die," she added, sounding frightened again.

"Well, that's not true," Jane said. She laughed. "My grandma used to frighten me and my brother stiff with stories like that when we were just a bit younger than you and Neil. She was a farmer's daughter, and she told us that one night she was going home down a lane when she saw this big, black dog standing in her path. She told it to move, but it didn't, and when she went up to it, she stepped right through it, and then it wasn't there any more."

"And did anybody die?" Emily asked.

"No. In fact, not long after she saw the dog, she met my grandpa and they got married, so she always said the black dog brought her luck. But you know . . . ," she gave Emily a mischievous grin, "I think she made it all up. She told good stories."

Emily managed to smile back. "Well, I suppose it's silly to think that a dog can make people die. But all the same, we saw something in the churchyard. We really did! And it wasn't like anything I've seen before."

On the Saturday morning after school had broken up for winter vacation, Neil persuaded Emily to help him set up the Agility course in the field. He had put all thoughts of the ghost dog out of his mind. The vacation was his best chance of getting Sam into training for the big Agility contest in Manchester, and Neil was determined to show Jane Hammond what a rescue dog could do.

"Where's Sam?" Emily asked, as they hauled planks into place. Usually by this time Sam was bounding around impatiently, hardly able to wait for the course to be ready.

Neil straightened up. "Don't say he's gone over to Jane's again! She'll kill me." He went off to look for Sam. Calling and whistling didn't do much good. Neil was beginning to think the worst when he decided to check under Sam's favorite bush at the bottom of the garden. To his surprise, the Border collie was there, lying with his nose on his paws, looking very drowsy.

"Had a good sleep?" Neil asked. "Wake up, Sam. What's the matter with you?"

Sam yawned at him.

"Are we training this morning?" Neil slapped his leg. "Come on, boy!"

With a long-suffering look, Sam hauled himself to his feet and followed Neil into the exercise field.

"I can't figure out what's the matter with him," Neil said to Emily. "He doesn't seem sharp at all this morning."

"Maybe he's thinking about his girlfriend," Emily said. While Neil was away she had finished building the course. "Come on, Sam! Pretend Delilah's waiting for you at the finish."

Neil took Sam over the course, with Emily timing

him, but the Border collie was even slower than the last time he had trained.

"This'll never do," said Neil, as Sam sat panting. "If he goes on like this there'll be no point in entering."

"He did do everything right," said Emily.

"Yes, but he's so slow. I can't understand it. OK, Sam, let's try again — and this time get a move on."

Sam began the course. At first, he was faster than before, and as Neil urged him on, he began to think that the problem had gone away.

The Border collie leapt through the tire without hesitation, but when he should have climbed up onto the dogwalk he swerved away, and stood with his head down. As Neil ran up to him, he coughed.

"Sam?" Neil said. "What's wrong, boy?" He knelt beside Sam, but the coughing had stopped, and the collie seemed no different from usual.

"What's the matter?" Emily asked.

"I don't know. Sam was coughing. Maybe he got something stuck in his throat — or maybe he's sick."

"There's Dad." Emily pointed to where Bob Parker was leaning on the gate watching the training. "Let's ask him."

Neil beckoned and Bob came through the gate and joined them. As he listened to what Neil told him, his hand rasped through stubble that was now almost long enough to be called a beard. "Oh, no. Don't tell me we've got a case of kennel cough."

"It can't be," Neil objected. "All the dogs who come here have had their injections. Sam has had his, too."

"Yes, but what we call kennel cough is a whole group of different diseases caused by a lot of different viruses. You can't vaccinate a dog against all of them. And if one dog goes down — it can infect all the others. We haven't had an outbreak of kennel cough here for three years."

"Should we take him to see Mike Turner?" Neil asked anxiously.

"Not now. But we'll keep an eye on him for the next day or two. And Neil, keep him away from the other dogs as much as you can, just in case."

"And from Delilah," Emily added.

"Don't!" Neil rolled his eyes. "I can just imagine what Jane would say if we gave her precious Delilah kennel cough!"

Bob Parker went straight to the kennel to check all the boarding dogs and the ones in the rescue center, but none of them were coughing.

"Thank goodness for that," he said to Neil, as they finished the job in the rescue block. "There's nothing worse than having to explain to an owner why their dog got sick while it was in your care. Still, keep Sam by himself for a few days, will you?"

"Sure," Neil said. He looked down at Tess, the little black poodle who was standing with her paws up against the wire of her pen, watching him expectantly. He fished out one of the dog treats he always carried and gave it to her. Tess snapped it up and, sharp-eyed, looked around for more.

"She's healthy enough," Bob said. "Especially now that we've had a chance to fatten her up."

"Did you find out any more about her owner?" Neil asked.

"Ann Barton? Not much. I got in touch with the owner of the apartment where she was living. She told them she was moving because she'd got a new job, but she didn't leave a forwarding address." He sighed. "It seems as if she did abandon Tess after all.

It's odd, because *someone* had obviously loved and looked after Tess."

"Will you look for a new owner now?"

"I'd better." He shook his head, frowning slightly. "But there's something about this that's not right at all."

For the next two days, Neil continued Sam's training. The Border collie's times improved, and Neil didn't notice him coughing again. He began to think that the problem, whatever it was, had cleared up, and he started to feel more confident. It was an important competition, but Neil thought Sam had a chance. If he could win, or even be placed, maybe Jane Hammond would admit that he was good enough for Delilah.

Neil also did his best to keep Sam at home. It was easier during the half-term week, when he could be with Sam for most of the day, but he wondered what would happen when he had to go back to school.

On Tuesday evening, the Parkers were eating dinner around the big wooden kitchen table. Sam was asleep in his basket. Neil was just scraping the last of his cauliflower out of his dish when the doorbell rang.

"I'll get it," Emily said.

She went out and came back a minute later with Jane Hammond just behind her. Jane looked flushed and furious. But Sam's here, Neil thought. What's eating her now?

"Hello, Jane," Carole said. "What can we do for you?"

"You can't do anything," Jane said. Her voice was shaking with anger. "It's too late now. The damage has already been done. I just knew this was going to happen!"

"What's wrong?" Bob asked.

"Wrong? I'll tell you what's wrong. Delilah is pregnant. She's going to have Sam's puppies!"

CHAPTER SIX

"Puppies!" Sarah bounced up and down on her chair with excitement. "Sam's puppies! Will Sam and Delilah get married now?"

Jane Hammond ignored her. "Mike Turner says Delilah's five to six weeks pregnant. The puppies are due in three weeks, and we had no idea. She's only just starting to show!"

Neil was forking food into his mouth almost automatically while he kept his eyes fixed on Jane. He could see how angry she was, and he understood why she didn't want Delilah mated with a nonpedigree dog. All the same he couldn't help feeling a thrill at the thought of Sam being a father.

"Five to six weeks?" Bob said. "That must be just after you moved in. Certainly before your party."

"Indeed. I said at the time that Sam had been hanging around! He didn't waste any time, did he?"

"I'm really sorry," Carole said. "I know what a problem it is for you. Sometimes pregnant dogs do take a long time to show. Why don't you sit down and let's talk it over? Neil, please get another chair."

Neil brought another chair up to the table, but Jane refused to sit down. "There's nothing to talk over. It's too late now." She dug her hands into the pockets of her jacket and hunched her shoulders. "There's nothing anybody can do."

"Well, we can help with the pups," Bob said. "You'll still be able to sell them, you know, as working dogs or pets. I can think of plenty of people who would be interested."

"I know. It's just that . . . well, I had hopes of setting up in business, and breeding dogs for show. Delilah's perfect for that."

"Well, it's not the end of the world," said Bob. "She's a young dog, isn't she?"

"Yes, this is her first litter. Oh . . ." Jane groped for the chair and sank into it, resting her elbows on the table and pushing her fingers into her hair. "All that fuss and bother," she said. "And it was too late all the time. You must think I'm a real pain."

"Don't be silly," Carole said. "We understand."

"We'll help when the pups are little," Emily said. "They'll be a lot of work."

"Sure," said Neil. "We'll come over whenever you want us to."

"Thanks." Jane raised her head and managed to smile. "That's good of you. To be honest, I'm feeling a bit scared. It's my first litter, you know, as well as Delilah's."

"In that case," Neil said, grinning, "you've come to the right place!"

The next morning, while he and Emily helped with the kennel work, Neil couldn't get Sam's pups out of his mind.

"How about that, Sam?" he said to the Border collie. Sam was trotting at Neil's heels as he crossed the courtyard with water bowls for the rescue center. "You're going to be a dad!"

Sam looked up at him, his ears pricked, and gave him a doggy grin.

"You're really pleased with yourself, aren't you, boy?" Neil said.

In the rescue center Neil found Emily, who had brought in the food bowls. She was crouched down inside Tess's pen; the little poodle was climbing over her enthusiastically, licking her face.

"Oh, she's lovely," Emily said. "Who could bear to go away and leave her behind?"

"Somebody did," said Neil. "This Ann Barton, who-ever she is." He put a water bowl down beside Tess and took the other to the Skye terrier in the pen next door. "That's the last one. Do you want to help with Sam's training?"

"Neil," said Emily, "listen." She gave Tess a final pat, got up, and left the pen, fastening the door carefully behind her. "Have you thought any more about the ghost?"

Neil shrugged. If he was honest, he hadn't thought about much except Sam for several days.

"Don't you think it matters?" Emily faced Neil and fixed her eyes on him. "Julie and I did see something in the churchyard. Do you believe me or not?"

Neil frowned. To buy some time, he led the way out of the rescue center. Emily was still watching him with a determined expression. Neil knew that she never gave up. And although she had some funny ideas sometimes, she wasn't stupid. If she said she'd seen something, then she probably had.

"OK," said Neil. "I believe you. But I don't believe it was a ghost."

"Then what do you think it was?" Emily was giving Neil the sort of look that Mr. Hamley sometimes gave him when he was being particularly stupid in class.

"A real dog?"

"Do you think so?" asked Emily. She thought for a moment and then said, "Well, if it is, I want to go and find it."

As soon as lunch was over, Neil and Emily set off for Compton on their bikes. Neil left Sam behind; there was no need any more to watch him all the time. And if there was a real dog hanging around the church, Neil didn't want it getting into a fight with Sam.

In daylight, the churchyard still looked a bit spooky. It surrounded the church, which was on a hill. The path wound upward between the gravestones and monuments. Dark, bushy yew trees cast shadows over it. Neil admitted to himself that Emily and Julie had been pretty brave to come up here in the evening with only Ben for company.

They left their bikes by the gate and walked up the path toward the church.

"What sort of dog are we looking for?" Neil asked. "A huge St. Bernard or a miniature poodle like Tess?"

Emily frowned, and shook dark hair out of her eyes. "It's not a joke, Neil. The shadow was pretty big." She held out a hand at about waist level. "About this high."

That didn't help much, Neil thought. The size of the shadow didn't necessarily tell them the size of the dog. But in his mind he was picturing something big. It was hard to imagine anyone being frightened by a dog as tiny as Tess.

Emily took Neil to where she and Julie had seen the shadow. On the way they looked in hollows under trees and behind the gravestones, but they didn't see a dog, or any sign that a dog had been there.

Emily stopped beside the statue of an angel. It towered over her with huge wings and flowing hair and robes and had an open book in its hands. It looked sad, maybe because its white marble was stained with bird droppings, and it had been badly weathered.

"It was here," she said.

"Show me exactly where you and Julie were standing."

Emily stood with half closed eyes, thinking, and then moved a few feet away from the statue.

"We were here," she said, "and it looked as if the dog was standing beside the angel. I suppose what we saw must have been a shadow cast on the angel — that would explain how it disappeared without making a noise!"

"And where was the light?" Neil asked, standing beside her.

"What?"

"The light. It was getting dark, remember. If there was a shadow, there must have been a light."

Emily concentrated in her effort to picture the scene. She waved an arm. "Near the church. It was coming from our right."

Neil looked at the church. There was a ground-level light illuminating a path leading from a side door. If he looked in a direct line from there to the angel, he could see that the dog itself must have been standing close to the door. He walked over to the place, examining the ground carefully.

"What are you looking for?" Emily asked.

"Footprints." Neil grinned as he remembered the Sherlock Holmes story that Mr. Hamley was reading to the class. "The footprints of a gigantic hound!"

But Neil wasn't Sherlock Holmes, and he couldn't see anything on the path or the springy grass beside it. It was several days since Emily had been here, and if there had been any marks they would have disappeared by now. Neil shrugged. "Nothing," he said. "But I guess if it stood here it was following you from around the back of the church."

Emily shivered. "Ugh!"

"I bet Ben scared it off. Let's go and look."

Neil set off along the path that led behind the church. Here the churchyard looked much older, with tombstones tilted at angles starting to sink into the earth and half-covered by moss and lichen. Neil would have thought that no one had disturbed it for years, except that not far away he could hear the sound of a lawn mower.

Emily caught up with him. "There's tons of places a dog could hide!"

She was right. The churchyard ended at a fence edged by trees and bushes. The only gap in the undergrowth was where the path led to a gate. Neil ran across the grass and looked over it. On the other side of the fence was a road leading steeply down the hill in the direction of the town and beyond that what looked like the back gardens of houses in the next road.

"I wonder if the dog comes from over there," Emily said.

"It might. If there is a dog hanging around here it must be getting food from somewhere."

Neil began to make his way along the line of bushes, peering underneath them and using a stick to poke into the darkest hollows. Emily tried calling, but there was no sound or movement in reply. Neil began to wonder if they were wrong after all.

As they moved along the fence, the sound of the mower got louder and it suddenly came into view from behind an enormous tomb, which looked like something out of a Dracula film. A young man was pushing it. He was tall and thin with floppy dark hair. Neil thought he looked vaguely familiar, but he couldn't remember where he'd seen him before. When he saw Neil and Emily he switched off the mower and stood up, wiping the back of his hand across his forehead.

"It's tiring work," he said. "Can I do something for you?"

"We were looking for . . ." Neil let his voice fade away. It sounded stupid to say you were looking for a ghost.

Emily wasn't as fussy. "We were looking for the ghost dog," she explained.

Neil expected the young man to laugh, but he didn't. "Oh, yeah, the ghost," he said. "I've heard about it. Have you found anything?"

"We don't really think it's a ghost," Neil told him hastily. "But we think there's something here. Em's seen it."

The young man smiled down at Emily. "What have you seen?"

Emily described how she and Julie had come up to the churchyard and seen the shadow on the statue of the angel, and how Ben had stood still, growling.

"Your dog thought something was there," the young man said. "That's interesting. Because a lot of people believe in ghosts, but I'm pretty sure that dogs don't!" He wiped one hand on his filthy jeans and held it out to them.

"I'm Gavin Thorpe," he said. "I'm the vicar here."

Now Neil remembered where he had seen him before — at the harvest festival — but he'd looked very different in his vicar's robes. Now he was wearing dirty blue jeans and a red sweater with holes in it. Neil wouldn't have expected to see a vicar dressed like that, or mowing his own churchyard, either.

"I'm Neil Parker," he said. "And this is my sister Emily. We're from King Street Kennels."

"Well, you would know all about dogs," Gavin said thoughtfully. "What do you think about all this?"

"We think it's a real dog," said Emily.

The vicar nodded. "I hope you're right. I'd like to get to the bottom of it, because I know it's frightening people."

"If it is a real dog," Neil said, "we ought to find it and take it to our rescue center, or find its proper owner."

"I suppose it might get savage and attack someone."

Neil had been thinking about the dog, not the harm it might do to anyone else, but he knew the vicar was right. "It wouldn't be the dog's fault," he said. "But if it's neglected, or starving — yes, it could turn on someone."

"Do you think you could keep a lookout for it?"

Emily asked. She flushed a little, and went on quickly, "We can't be here all the time, and next week we'll be back at school, but you're always around, aren't you?"

Gavin laughed. "One way or another, yes. And I'll certainly keep my eyes open. Maybe I could try putting some food and water out. And if I see anything, I'll give you a call."

"That would be great!" Neil felt a lot better. The vicar didn't think they were being foolish, and he was willing to do something to help. "If there is a dog, we'll look after it."

"Good." Gavin switched on the mower again and raised a hand as they said good-bye. As Neil and Emily set off back to their bikes, he went on trimming the grass around Dracula's tomb.

After the visit to the church, Neil felt he'd done his duty as far as the ghost dog was concerned. He didn't have to feel guilty about giving all his time to Sam. The Agility contest in Manchester was in less than three weeks, and Sam had to be in top form if he stood any chance of winning it.

Neil realized that Delilah wouldn't be able to compete because she was expecting puppies. That gave Sam a better chance. It was even more important to work hard at his training. Neil was still determined to prove to Jane what a good dog Sam was.

On the Thursday night before the contest, Neil was still uneasy that Sam wasn't as fast as he had once been. He didn't seem as sharp even though he was getting a clear round almost every time.

Toward the end of the training session, Bob Parker stood watching while Neil worked with Sam. The dog trotted up the seesaw, paused to let it tilt over, and scrambled down the other side and up the steps. Neil encouraged Sam as he ran for the finish.

"Perfect!" he said. "Well done, boy!"

He was going to ask his father what Sam's time had been when he looked at the dog more closely. Instead of coming up for his reward of a treat from Neil's pocket, Sam was standing with his feet apart, head lowered, and coughing. Neil crouched down beside him. "What's the matter, boy?"

Bob strode over to stand beside them.

"Is this what he did before?"

"Yes, but it sounds worse this time."

Sam's coughing was going on longer and it sounded deep inside his chest.

"There's something wrong!" Neil said, trying not to panic.

Bob tried to open Sam's jaws and have a look as he had before, but the Border collie backed away. He coughed again, and then flopped down on the grass, panting.

"What is it, Dad?"

"I don't know. Not kennel cough, because none of

the other dogs has it. Maybe he's picked up a virus but hasn't managed to pass it on." He put a hand on Neil's shoulder. "Don't look so worried! I'm sure he'll be fine. All the same," he added slowly, "I think it's time we had a word with Mike Turner."

CHAPTER SEVEN

Mike Turner came up to King Street Kennels the following afternoon for one of his regular visits. He was still there when Neil got home from school. Neil raced over to where he could see the vet talking to his father outside Kennel Block One.

"Hi, Mike. Have you seen Sam yet?" he asked urgently.

"Not yet," Mike said. "Your dad told me about him, but I thought I'd wait for you before I examined him."

"He's in the kitchen," said Bob.

Bubbling over with impatience and worry, Neil led the way into the house. Emily was already in the kitchen, bending over Sam's basket and stroking his head. Sam got out of the basket as Neil came in, and stood there alertly. As far as Neil could tell, he was perfectly normal.

Mike Turner squatted down in front of him and rumpled his ears. "What's the matter, boy?" he asked. "It's a pity he can't tell us, isn't it?" He peered down Sam's throat, and moved his hands carefully over the collie's chest. Then he pulled out a stethoscope and listened through it while Neil and Emily watched anxiously. Sam, sitting now, looked as if he was enjoying all the attention.

At last Mike put the stethoscope away and sat back on his heels.

"Well," he said, "there's no blockage in his wind-pipe, I'm sure of that. He may have picked up an infection, but I doubt it. There may be nothing wrong at all, but I think you'd better bring him down to the clinic so that I can give him a thorough checkup."

Neil didn't know whether to feel reassured or not. He had hoped that Mike Turner would have given him an answer right away about what was wrong with Sam.

"When can we come?" he asked.

"Oh . . . Monday after school," Mike said. "Keep an eye on him over the weekend, and let me know if there are any changes."

"Can he still do the Agility contest?" Neil felt desperate. If Sam couldn't compete, his chance of impressing Jane before the pups were born would be ruined.

Mike thought for a minute. "You'll both be disappointed if I say no, won't you? Keep him quiet beforehand, and if he shows that he doesn't want to do it, pull him out. Sam will know what he can do, better than we do."

When Mike had said his good-byes, Neil showed him out through the front door. As he was going back to the kitchen, the telephone rang. Neil picked up the receiver.

"Hello, King Street Kennels," he said.

"Hello." It was a young woman's voice; Neil didn't recognize it. "This is Ann Barton speaking. I think you have my dog."

"Tess? Little black poodle?"

"That's right." The caller sounded really relieved. "I didn't even know she was missing."

Neil couldn't make sense of that. Shrugging, he asked, "When can you come and pick her up?"

Ann Barton laughed. "That'll be a little difficult. You see, I'm calling from New York."

"What?"

Ann laughed again. "I'm sorry. I guess it comes as a shock to you. But I was sitting here in my apartment, surfing the Net with a couple of friends, and just for fun I tried a search for anything to do with Compton. I came up with your website, and I couldn't believe it when I saw Tess's details there."

Neil wanted to jump up and down and cheer. It worked! It really worked! All the way to the United States.

"The firm I work for sent me over here. I'll be away for about a year, and I knew if I brought Tess she would hate it. And she'd have to go into quarantine when we came back. So my mother offered to look after her. She lives in Shepton, so what Tess is doing in Compton I can't imagine."

"Maybe she tried to go home," Neil said. Shepton was a village about fifteen miles from Compton; Tess must have been really brave to have come so far by herself.

The door of the office opened, and Carole came out. She looked inquiringly at Neil, who handed her the phone. He couldn't stop grinning. "Tess's owner," he said.

"Oh, good," Carole said, taking the phone and introducing herself. Neil watched as she listened and her face changed. "You're calling from *where?*"

Neil went back to the kitchen to tell his father and Emily all about it. Carole followed him after a few minutes.

"What's going to happen to Tess?" Emily asked.

"I've got Ann's mother's phone number," said Carole. "I'll give her a call and arrange for her to pick up Tess. The poor woman must be frantic. She obviously hadn't dared tell Ann that Tess was missing."

"So Tess wasn't abandoned after all," Bob said. "That's good to know. You did a great job with the website, Neil."

"Thanks." Neil looked over at Sam, who was back in his basket. "Now all we have to worry about is the contest tomorrow."

The Parkers were standing by the sidelines of the arena where the Agility competition would take place. The course looked fearsome; Neil had walked through it earlier, and as usual it had made him nervous. It was easily the longest and most demanding course Sam had ever tackled, and Neil wasn't sure how he would cope.

Sam on the other hand looked just as he always did: bright and interested and enjoying the excitement and all the people. Neil was watching him carefully for any sign of illness because he would do as Mike Turner said and not run him if Sam seemed at all unhappy.

It was a cold day heavy with clouds. The wind felt damp. Wet ground would make the course even harder, Neil thought, but so far the rain had held off.

"All right, boy?" he said. "Should we go for it?"

Sam sprang to his feet, tail wagging. Bob laughed. "Not much doubt there," he said.

The loudspeaker called the competitors for Sam's class. The rest of the family wished them luck, and Neil began to lead Sam toward the entrance to the ring. Before he got there, Jane Hammond appeared out of the crowd.

"I'm green with envy," she said. "Delilah should have been in this."

Neil felt himself going red. "Sorry —"

Jane was smiling. "Not your fault. Good luck, anyway."

"How is Delilah?"

"Big and heavy and restless. She looks as if she's got a whole pack in there. I think she'll be glad when it's all over, but there's a few more days to go yet."

"You'll let us know, won't you?" Neil asked. "I'm dying to see Sam's pups."

"Yes, of course. Better go now, though, or you'll miss your class."

Neil joined the other dogs and owners who were milling around the entrance to the ring. He recognized one or two of the dogs, including the Airedale that Sam had beaten into third place in the last competition in Padsham. Neil's excitement was growing. With Delilah out of the running, maybe Sam had a real chance of winning.

The Airedale was the first dog to go. He did well, but missed one of the contact points and took a penalty. The next, a Doberman, got a clear round but obviously wasn't fast enough, even though his owner did her best to urge him on. The third, a young German shepherd, missed the seesaw entirely.

Neil's mouth was dry as he watched, trying to ignore the pounding of his heart. So far none of the dogs had done as well as Sam at his best. Would he be at his best today?

Sam was the last dog to go. Neil swallowed nervously as he brought him up to the starting line, waiting for the signal.

"This is it, boy," he murmured. "Let's show them all how good you are! Go, Sam! *Go!*"

Sam leapt away as soon as Neil released his collar. He went straight through the fixed tire and raced eagerly for the bridge. He touched the yellow contact

point. Over the bridge, which was built above a make-believe pond. Down . . . contact point . . . and away. Down the tunnel and out the other end.

"Come on, Sam!" Neil urged, running alongside. "You can do it!"

Somewhere at the back of his mind Neil could hear the crowd shouting encouragement, but he tried to shut out the noise. He had to concentrate, as hard as he'd ever done, and give Sam all the help he could.

His nervousness grew as the Border collie took each of the obstacles correctly. The course was hard. One mistake would make all the difference between winning and losing.

At about the halfway mark, Neil felt the cold spatter of rain on his face. He groaned, but the rain didn't seem to bother Sam.

His dog worked the correct way through the poles, touched the next contact point, its yellow surface already slick with rain, and headed toward the second fixed tire. Neil caught his breath, but Sam didn't hesitate. Through the tire, landing neatly on the wet ground. Up the seesaw. As it tilted he looked a bit unsteady, but he recovered. Sam paused on the contact point at the bottom and then went bounding up the steps and down, and gathered himself for the final jump and the race to the finish line.

Neil couldn't help shouting "Yes!" even before he reached it. Sam had a clear round and a good time. Even if he didn't win, he'd run his best course ever.

But just as Sam reached the finish, he began to stagger. He crossed the line and seemed to crumple, fighting for his balance on legs that buckled under him. A gasp came from the crowd as he fell. Neil pounded up to him, expecting him to spring up. But he didn't. He lay on his side, not moving. Words sounded from the loudspeaker but Neil didn't hear them. He looked down at the dog's limp body. Sam didn't seem to be breathing.

CHAPTER EIGHT

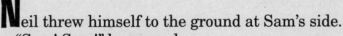

Neil threw himself to the ground at Sam's side.

"Sam! Sam!" he gasped.

He reached out for the collie, wanting to shake life back into him, desperate to do something, but not knowing what. Then, as he bent down close to Sam, he realized that he was still breathing, very fast and shallow, scarcely moving his chest at all.

"Sam, wake up!" he pleaded.

A firm hand closed over his arm, drawing him back a little. It was his father.

"What happened? What's wrong?" Neil asked desperately.

"Steady now. Let's take a look."

Bob crouched beside Sam and laid a hand lightly on his chest. Dazed, Neil looked up. Emily was standing beside him, her face turned white. Not far away, his mother had her arms around Sarah, who was sobbing with her face buried in Carole's coat. A ring of concerned people stood around them; Neil saw that Jane was there, too.

A middle-aged woman came briskly out of the crowd and knelt down beside Sam. To his relief, Neil recognized her tall figure and cropped gray hair: Jill Walker, a vet from Padsham.

"What happened?" she asked.

"He collapsed," Neil told her. "He'd just finished the Agility course. He was fantastic . . . is he going to die?"

"Can't say yet."

Her no-nonsense manner calmed Neil, but his stomach was still churning as if he was going to be sick. He wanted to yell at Jill and his father, to tell them to do something quickly, not to let Sam die. The collie was still lying as he had fallen, and Neil was terrified that at any second the shallow breathing would stop.

Jill Walker put her hand on the inside of Sam's thigh and looked as if she were waiting for something. At last she said, "I think it's his heart. His pulse is very weak."

"You mean he had a heart attack?" said Neil.

"No. Dogs don't get heart attacks, not like we do. He's fainted. Running the course put too much strain on his heart." She relaxed and smiled at Neil.

"I don't think he'll die. But you should get him to Mike Turner as quickly as you can. Can you leave right away? He's going to need a lot of care. Keep him warm, too."

She got up, shook hands with Bob, and vanished into the crowd again. Neil found he was shaking with relief. He felt tears on his face and scrubbed them away angrily with his sleeve. "I should never have made him do it," he said.

"You didn't make him," said Bob. "Sam was loving it. He always does."

"He was amazing," said Emily.

Neil gently tried to lift Sam.

"Let me take him, Neil," Bob said, placing a hand on Neil's shoulder. Bob crouched down and gathered Sam up in his strong arms. The collie lay limp, his coat dappled with rain. Now that the emergency was over the crowd was melting away; Jane Hammond came up to them.

"Can I help?" she asked.

"No, thanks," said Bob. "We'll take him straight to Mike Turner."

"Then I'll call and warn him that you're on your way."

"Good idea. Tell him that Jill Walker said it was his heart."

Jane hurried off, and the Parkers started to follow Bob out of the ring. Just then, the loudspeaker crackled into life. Emily tugged Neil's sleeve.

"It's your results."

"It doesn't matter, even if —"

The loudspeaker interrupted him.

"First — Neilsboy Puppy Patrol Sam!"

For a few seconds, Neil stood transfixed. Sam had won. He was a champion at an important show. But he was also Neil's best friend, and Neil knew that mattered more than anything. He turned and hurried after his father.

The drive back to Compton and Mike Turner's clinic seemed to take forever. Neil sat in the back of the Range Rover with Sam's head in his lap. Sam remained still, his eyes closed, but Neil thought that his breathing was stronger.

Mike Turner was waiting for them on the steps of the clinic. When the Range Rover pulled up he opened the door and lifted Sam out.

"I was at home," he said. "It's a good thing Jane called me. Let's get this fella into the intensive care unit."

The Parkers followed him inside. Carole kept Sarah with her in the waiting room so Mike wouldn't be too crowded.

Mike laid Sam on the examination table in the intensive care unit. Warned by Jane's phone call, he had already set up the X-ray equipment.

"I need to look at his heart," he said, as he adjusted the machine. "I wish I'd done it sooner." He sounded angry with himself.

"It's not your fault," Bob said. "Sam had been resting when you examined him."

Mike shook his head impatiently. He pressed the
switch and the machine whirred.

"Will Sam need an operation?" Neil asked.

"No." Mike shook his head. "You can't operate on a
dog for heart disease."

"Then he *will* die!"

"Did I say that?" Neil was encouraged to see that
though Mike was looking serious he wasn't anything
like as upset as he became if he knew he was going
to lose one of his animal patients. "No, Neil, what
happens to Sam now is going to depend on you."

Suddenly Neil felt brighter. He straightened up.

There was something he could do after all; he didn't have to feel so horribly helpless. "Just tell me what he needs," he said.

"Let's have a look at this X-ray first," said Mike.

It seemed like an eternity to Neil while Mike fiddled with the machine. Neil stood quietly, stroking Sam's head. The collie looked more comfortable now, more as if he was naturally asleep.

"I think he'll be all right," Emily whispered.

Neil didn't know if she was trying to reassure him or herself.

At last Mike extracted the photographic film from the X-ray machine and pored over it carefully. Neil and Emily waited in an agony of impatience.

"OK," Mike said, just as Neil was deciding he couldn't wait any longer. "This is it, Neil. I'm going to tell you the truth because I think you can take it, and you'll need to know if you're going to help Sam."

Neil nodded. His heart was heavy in his chest. "Anything," he said, and cleared his throat. "I'll do anything."

"Sam's heart is damaged. He's very unlucky, because it's an unusual condition in Border collies, and Sam's still a relatively young dog."

"How did it happen?" Neil asked. "Was he born like that?"

"And will he pass it on to his puppies?" Emily added.

Mike shook his head. "No, it's not genetic. Pups

that are born with a damaged heart don't usually live very long. So it's highly unlikely that Sam will pass a problem on to Delilah's pups — though you can be sure I'll give them all a thorough checkup! Sam probably strained his heart when he was younger — maybe even when he was abandoned."

"Then why haven't we noticed it before?" Neil asked.

"Because dogs' hearts can expand a little to make up for the damage. Look at the X-ray." He held it up against the light so that Neil and Emily could see. "His heart's pretty enlarged — there, look. But today he was doing more than he could cope with, his heart couldn't push the blood through fast enough, and that's when he fainted."

Neil swallowed and squared his shoulders.

"This means no more Agility competitions, doesn't it?" he asked.

"Yes, Neil," Mike said. "I'm afraid it does." He paused and then went on more briskly. "That's the bad news. The good news is that he's not going to die just yet, and if you manage him properly he will probably live for several years."

Neil thought of all the good times he'd had training Sam and competing with him. He thought about how Sam had loved it. He thought of the champion dog he could have been.

"He won today," he said. "He really went out with a bang!"

Mike smiled. "That's good to hear. Now, I'll keep

him overnight, just to make sure he gets a good rest, but I expect he can go home tomorrow. I'll prepare some diet sheets for him — he needs a salt-free diet. And I'll prescribe him a drug to stabilize his heart rate."

Neil looked down at Sam and stroked him again.

"Hear that, boy?" he said. "We're going to look after you."

As if Sam had understood, he opened his eyes and his tail thumped once on the examination table.

"He's awake!" said Emily.

"He'll be better off asleep just for now," Mike said. "Come on, let's get him into one of the cages. Then he'll have to rest."

The intensive care unit had special heated cages with sheepskin pads for the dogs to sleep on. Neil lifted Sam into one of them, and the Border collie settled down again with his nose on his paws. Neil gave him a farewell pat.

"You're the best, boy," he said. "You always will be."

It was dark when the Parkers arrived home. They were surprised to see Jane Hammond's car parked in the driveway. The security lights were on around the house and the kennel blocks, and there was a light in the kitchen. When Neil went in he saw Kate McGuire and Jane sitting at the kitchen table, drinking coffee.

Jane sprang to her feet. "Is he all right?"

Bob told her what had happened at Mike Turner's while Kate, who had been looking after the kennels while the Parkers were away at the show, made more coffee.

"Jane told me all about it," she said to Neil. "I'm really sorry."

"At least Sam's coming home," said Neil. "That's the important thing."

"Yes — this place wouldn't be the same without Sam."

Jane took something out of her pocket and held it out to Neil. It was a bright red ribbon.

"This is Sam's," she said. "I picked it up for him."

Neil took it and played with it in his fingers. "Thanks. I'll put it up here," he said, fixing it to the kitchen corkboard. "Then Sam can see it as soon as he gets home."

He was feeling tightness in his throat again. It wouldn't take much to make him start crying, there in the kitchen in front of everybody. When the telephone rang it was the ideal excuse to get out of there.

In the hallway, Neil picked up the phone. "King Street Kennels."

"Is Jane there?" The caller sounded frantic. Neil recognized the voice as Richard Hammond's. "I've got to talk to her. It's Delilah. Tell Jane that Delilah's puppies are coming!"

CHAPTER NINE

Neil went back into the kitchen and gave the message to Jane. She stared at him, color draining from her face. "What? She can't be! She's got days to go yet!"

"Puppies often come a few days early," Bob said comfortably. "It's not unusual."

Jane shot out into the hallway to take the call.

"Richard sounded scared stiff," Neil said, laughter bubbling up inside him. A few minutes before, Neil had thought he would never feel like laughing again.

"Will Delilah be all right?" Emily asked anxiously.

"I should think so," her father reassured her. "She's a fine, healthy dog."

Sarah was bouncing around the kitchen, singing,

"Puppies, puppies, lots of puppies!" For once, Neil didn't blame her for being excited.

Jane came back into the kitchen a few moments later. She looked as if she was in a real state. "I've got to go," she said.

"Will you be OK?" Carole asked.

"I don't know — I've never done this before. Oh, and I forgot to tell Richard to call Mike Turner. Can I do it from here?"

"I've got a better idea," said Carole. "I'll call Mike, and Bob will go home with you and give you a hand with Delilah until Mike gets there. How about that?"

A smile spread across Jane's face. "Oh, would you?"

"No problem," said Bob.

"Can we come?" Neil asked. "Em and me? It's the first time we'll have seen pups being born."

"And me!" begged Sarah.

Bob hesitated, tugging his beard. It was a real beard now, all brown and curly. Neil thought his father looked like a kindly pirate.

"OK. But not you, Sarah," said Carole. "This could go on until way past your bedtime."

Sarah started to sulk and stomped off. Bob put on the coat he had taken off minutes before and beckoned to Neil and Emily. Jane was desperately impatient to leave, and far too nervous to drive, so everyone piled into the Parkers' Range Rover and set off for Old Mill Farm.

When they arrived, Jane led them around the back of the house and through a door into a scullery. The walls were whitewashed and the floor was made of flagstones. On one side were a sink and a washing machine and dryer and an enormous freezer. The other end of the room had been arranged for Delilah to give birth.

There was a whelping box with an infrared heat lamp and a thick pad of newspaper at the bottom. Delilah lay there on her side, with Richard Hammond crouching beside her. Against the wall was a table with equipment spread out on it.

Richard sprang up as the Parkers entered.

"Thank goodness you're back!" he said to Jane. "Bob!" He grabbed Bob's hand and shook it enthusiastically. "Tell us what's happening. She doesn't seem to be getting anywhere."

Jane knelt beside Delilah and started to stroke her head. Neil thought that Delilah looked a lot calmer than either of her owners. He and Emily stood to one side while Bob squatted down to examine her. As Neil watched, he saw a muscular ripple pass across Delilah's swollen abdomen, where the pups were waiting to be born. Delilah was panting rapidly.

Bob grinned. "She's in second-stage labor," he said. "How long has she been like this?"

Richard checked his watch. "About half an hour."

"There should be fun and games soon, then."

Neil and Emily stood back where they could see what was going on without getting in the way. The ripples down Delilah's body were stronger and faster. After a few minutes Bob said, "Here we go."

At first, Neil wasn't sure what he was seeing. A shape was appearing from Delilah's hindquarters: something tiny that looked almost as if it were wrapped in a plastic bag. Suddenly it slid out onto the newspaper. Delilah twisted around and sniffed it suspiciously.

"Come on, girl," Bob said. "Get on with it."

"That's a puppy?" Emily said disbelievingly.

Bob grinned at her. "You didn't think they came out all furry? Come on, Delilah," he added to the collie.

"She doesn't know what to do!" Jane said anxiously. "Will the puppy die?"

"No," Bob said. He was calm and reassuring. "We'll

just have to give her a bit of help. Do you have a towel?"

Richard gave him one from the table. Bob used it to pick up the tiny shape; Neil could see the head and tucked-up paws, very still underneath the substance that wrapped it.

"This is a kind of bag," Bob said, "that the puppy grows inside. Now we've got to get rid of it." He broke the covering and a watery liquid spilled over his hands and onto the newspaper. Holding the puppy's head down, he cleaned its nose and mouth to make sure it could breathe. Then he put the pup in front of Delilah. The collie sniffed it inquisitively, then nuzzled it and began to lick away the rest of the membrane that covered it.

Jane had a hand over her mouth. "It's not moving!"

The puppy itself answered her with a faint mewing sound. Jane gasped, and Neil felt his face breaking into a wide grin. Delilah licked her first pup a little more and bit through the cord, which had fed it inside her. Then she gently nudged it around so that it could fasten onto one of her teats. It started to suck, feebly at first and then more vigorously.

"Wow!" Neil said. "That is absolutely the greatest thing I've ever seen!"

"We're not finished yet," said Bob. "There are more on the way."

After that, everything seemed to happen quickly. With the second puppy, Delilah licked the pup affectionately and nudged it toward a teat. Bob kept an eye on her and made sure she didn't accidentally squash one of the pups, but there wasn't much more for him to do.

As the fifth puppy was appearing, there was a tap on the scullery door and Mike Turner walked in. At first everybody was too intent on Delilah to notice him, until he squatted down beside Bob and said, "You don't look as if you need me."

"She's doing fine," Bob said. "No problems so far."

Neil glanced at the clock on the wall and was astonished to realize that two hours had passed since they had arrived at Old Mill Farm. It had only seemed like ten minutes!

Mike watched as Delilah took care of the fifth puppy, and when it was busy sucking he leaned over and gently examined Delilah.

"I think she's finished," he said. "Good girl. Well done." To Jane, he added, "I'm sorry I didn't get here sooner, but I couldn't leave Sam until I was sure he was stable."

Jane nodded. "Don't worry," she said. "Bob was marvelous."

"All part of the service," said Bob, grinning.

Now that the pups were all safely born, Neil and Emily came closer to the whelping box to have a good look at Delilah and her litter. She was lying on her side, half-curled around the pups, which were still sucking at her teats.

"They're beautiful," said Neil.

Emily's eyes were shining. "And so tiny!" she said.

Delilah looked drowsy; her eyes were closing.

"She'll have a good sleep now," said Mike. "She'll be tired out — it's not called labor for nothing, you know!"

"And what should we do next?" Richard asked.

"You can leave her alone now. Just keep an eye on her. If you leave the light on in here it won't bother her, and it's easier for you if you want to check her in the night. I'll look in again tomorrow."

"And we'll be going, too," said Bob. "It's been a long day."

"I can't thank you enough," said Jane. She looked down at Delilah and the litter for a moment, and then turned to Neil. "Listen," she went on, "I know you've had a problem with Sam. I'm really sorry things have turned out so badly. Would you like to have one of these pups?"

Neil stared at her. He couldn't believe she had said that. The pups were great, but *Sam* was his dog. Did Jane really think that any puppy in the world could make up for Sam?

"No," he said. "You don't understand. Sam's mine." His voice was rising. "He'll be all right. He's not going to die! He needs me. I don't want another dog!" By the time he had finished he was shouting.

His father said, "Neil —"

Jane started to say, "I didn't mean . . ."

Neil didn't want to listen to either of them. All his fears and worries about Sam rose up like a heavy, black cloud. He spun around and dashed out of the scullery, crashing the door shut behind him.

Neil ran into the darkness away from the farmhouse and across the field. He was sobbing as he pounded along, head down, not looking where he was going. His fists were clenched. Afraid that someone would follow him, he kept on running until his foot caught in a rabbit hole and he fell right down on the grass.

Just for a minute, his head on his crooked arm, he shed the tears for Sam he'd been keeping in all day, ever since his dog collapsed at the end of the Agility course. But Neil knew that didn't help. Soon he sat up, rubbing his face, and saw in the moonlight that he was not far away from the gap in the hedge that led from the Hammonds' land to the Parkers' own exercise field.

Slowly he got to his feet, pushed through the hedge, and jogged across the exercise field toward the house. At the gate, he stopped. There were lights in the house; his mother would be there, and Kate might have stayed on. Neil didn't want to talk to either of them, or anyone else.

He walked quietly through the garden and saw that his bike was leaning against the house. Even more quietly, he pushed it through the side gate and along the drive. He wanted to be by himself for a while; if he got into trouble later, that was just too bad.

Neil was riding into Compton before he really thought about where he meant to go. The town center was brightly lit with street lamps and the lights from cafés that were still open. But the churchyard, when he rode toward the entrance, was in darkness.

Neil braked, brought his bike to a halt, and pushed it through the churchyard gate. Maybe now, in pitch darkness, he'd finally find out the truth about the ghost dog. He left the bike at the gate but took his bike's headlight with him and walked slowly up the path.

Security lights illuminated the church itself, but beyond them were the shadows of bushes and gravestones. Neil thought they looked like crouching animals.

"Here, boy! Here!" he called softly.

There was no reply. Neil made his way toward the back of the church and across the grass toward the gate and the lane. His light cast a wavering pool around his feet. He called out again but heard nothing except his own breathing and the cry of a night bird.

He was beginning to feel cold. Going home seemed like a very good idea. Neil moved down the line of shrubs bordering the fence and began working his

way back across the grass. He was passing the
church again when he heard a rustling behind him.
He froze.

Just in front of him was the statue of the angel
glimmering in the night. Cast upon it, seeming to
stand in front of Neil and block his way, was the
shadow of an enormous black dog.

CHAPTER TEN

Very slowly, Neil turned around. Standing on the path behind him, lit by the ground-level light by the side door, was a black Labrador. An ordinary big dog, and no ghost, but solidly real.

"Good dog," Neil said quietly. "Stay, boy."

The dog did not move. Neil took a step forward, and at once the dog started backing away but stopped when he stopped.

"Don't be frightened, boy. I won't hurt you."

He tried again to get closer to the dog, and again the animal retreated until he was backed up against a clump of bushes. Neil stopped again. He wasn't sure what to do. If the Labrador slipped away into the shrubbery he might never find him again.

Moving as carefully as he could, so as not to startle the dog, Neil knelt down. Hoping the Labrador wasn't vicious, he slipped out one of the dog treats he always carried in his pocket and held it out flat on his palm.

"Here, boy. Good dog."

The dog eyed him but did not come to take the treat. He didn't look wild, but Neil knew there was a risk. Talking quietly, Neil flicked the dog treat toward the Labrador. It landed among the leaves near the dog's front paws, and he snuffled around until he found it. Neil slid another onto his hand. "Here, boy. You must be hungry."

The Labrador looked thin, as if he had been living wild for some time. Neil thought how much better looked-after he would be in the rescue center, if only he could get him there. And that made him realize another problem: even if the Labrador came to him, how would he manage to get him home with no collar and leash and no transportation except his bike?

He flipped the second treat between himself and the dog, and after a short hesitation the Labrador came and snatched it up. Neil was almost sure by now that he wasn't hostile. He was probably more nervous than Neil himself.

"That's it, boy. Come on," he said, holding the third biscuit out on his hand again.

This time, cautiously, the dog took it from him, looking at Neil with dark, sad eyes; his mouth felt soft. Neil patted his head and fondled his ears.

"Good boy. Well done," he said.

A new voice just behind him said, "Here." Neil never knew what kept him from screaming, but he stayed calm as he saw a hand reaching out of the darkness clutching a collar. Neil took it and fastened it around the neck of his new friend. Once it was secure, and he could grip it, he turned round to see Gavin Thorpe, the vicar, standing behind him.

"You had me scared stiff!" he whispered.

Gavin grinned. "Sorry," he said. "I didn't want to startle the dog."

"But it's OK to startle me?"

"Sorry," the vicar repeated. "Ever since we talked the other day I've been keeping a lookout, and I bought the collar in case I found him. And a leash, too." He pulled the leash out of his pocket and snapped it onto the collar. "Now what do we do?" he asked.

Neil gave the Labrador another pat, and another treat, before he got to his feet. "We call my dad," he said, "and put this ghost into the rescue center."

Gavin drove the dog and Neil home in his scruffy old car, with Neil's bike in the trunk.

"I wonder what his name is," he said, when they were on the road heading through Compton.

"We'd better give him one," said Neil.

"How about Jet?" Gavin suggested. "He's black,

and he's fast, or he couldn't have stayed hidden for so long."

"Jet it is," said Neil, as he twisted around to talk to the dog in the back of the car. "You're Jet, OK?"

As soon as the vicar's car turned into the driveway of King Street Kennels, Neil saw his mother running down the steps to meet him. As Neil got out she gave him a shake and then hugged him.

"Never give me such a scare again!" she said.

Neil wriggled out of the hug. "Sorry, Mom," he said. With a flourish he opened the back door of the car. "Meet Jet, the black ghost dog of Compton!"

Jet had decided that he liked the vicar's car, and it took some coaxing to get him out. By this time Bob and Emily had joined the group in the driveway. Emily crouched down and made friends with Jet, while Gavin introduced himself.

"What will happen to Jet now?" he asked.

"Well," said Bob, "we'll put him in a pen in the rescue center, and we'll try to find his previous owner. If we don't have any luck, we'll find a new home for him."

Gavin was looking down thoughtfully at the Labrador.

"And if you can't?"

"The council allows us three months, and after that the dog would have to be destroyed. Mind you," Bob added quickly, "that's never happened yet to a dog at King Street Kennels."

"That's dreadful," said Gavin, caressing Jet's head. "Just suppose . . . if you don't trace his owner . . . do you think I could have him?"

"Hey, great!" said Neil.

"I don't see why not," said Bob.

"I just feel he belongs at the vicarage," Gavin said. "Especially if he's been hanging around there for weeks. Hey, Jet, do you want to be the vicarage dog?"

He patted Jet again, and the dog slurped a wet tongue over his hand. His mournful eyes had grown brighter. Neil laughed. "I think we might call that a yes."

He and Emily grinned at each other, while their
dad and the vicar discussed details. If it hadn't been
for them, Neil thought, the people of Compton would
still be haunted by the shadow of a friendly black
Labrador. But now all the stories would have to
stop — the vicar wanted to adopt the terrifying
ghost dog!

Neil saw that Emily was looking thoughtful.
"What's up, Em?" he asked.

"Well," she said, "if Gavin hadn't said he wanted
Jet, I was going to call Jake Fielding at the *Compton
News*." She sighed. "It would have made a great
story!"

When Neil woke up the following day, everything
was quiet. He realized his mother had let him sleep
late. He washed hurriedly, pulled on some clothes,
and went downstairs.

The front door was open, and Neil could hear
voices coming from that direction. He went to see
what was going on.

A small, red car was parked in the driveway, and
Carole was talking to a tall, gray-haired woman who
was standing beside it. The woman had Tess in her
arms.

"I can't tell you how grateful I am," she said. "Ann
would have been so upset if she'd come home and
found that Tess was missing."

This must be Mrs. Barton, Neil thought, Ann Barton's mother, who was supposed to be looking after Tess. He went down the steps and joined his mother.

"This is my son, Neil," Carole said. "He put Tess's information on our website."

"I'm so glad you did," Mrs. Barton said. She shook hands with Neil. She was very well-dressed, and Neil thought she didn't really look like a dog person. Still, Tess seemed content enough to be with her, and as bright and perky as ever. "Tess is such a little dog," she went on. "I'd no idea she would be brave enough to come all the way to Compton."

"Well, if she goes missing again," Carole said, "get in touch with us. And it might be a good idea to get her a collar tag with your phone number."

Mrs. Barton looked embarrassed. "Yes, I will," she promised. "I'll do it today."

With more thanks, she got into her car and started it up.

"I hope she knows what she's doing," Neil said apprehensively.

"She'll be OK. And . . . ," Carole waved a check under Neil's nose, "she gave us a really generous donation for the rescue center."

They watched as the bright red car edged its way out of the driveway.

"Maybe we should call her in a few days," Neil suggested. "To make sure Tess has settled down."

"Good idea."

As the red car disappeared, Mike Turner's Range

Rover turned into the driveway and stopped. Mike got out, followed by Sam. The Border collie looked just as he always did, bright and alert. Neil knelt beside him and hugged him.

"Sam!" he exclaimed. "Sam, you're home!"

Sam licked his face and his ear. For a minute Neil just held him, feeling him warm and alive. He was so glad to have his friend back that he couldn't think of anything to say. He just grinned up at Mike and his mother, and then had to find a tissue and blow his nose hard.

Everybody went into the kitchen, where Carole made coffee and Neil helped himself to cereal and milk. Mike put a folder of papers onto the kitchen table.

"That's for you, Neil. I've made you some notes about how you should manage Sam — exercise and so on — and there are diet sheets. I've brought you a packet of special formula to give him now, and you can also cook him fresh meat and vegetables yourself. The main thing to remember is absolutely no salt. And there's a drug to stabilize his heart — you can mix that in with his food." He put the packets on the table along with the folder.

Neil stopped spooning his cereal to examine them. There would be a lot to remember, but he would do it. Nothing was too much trouble for Sam.

While he was reading Mike's notes, the outside

door opened, and Emily and Sarah came in. Sarah squealed and ran over to Sam.

"Be gentle with him," Mike said.

Sarah nodded, and sat on the floor beside Sam, petting him.

"Mommy," she said, "is it time to go and see Sam's puppies?"

"Almost," Carole said patiently. "As soon as Daddy comes in." She looked at Neil. "Jane came over first thing this morning to get her car. She invited us over to see the pups." She hesitated and then added, "You don't have to go, Neil, if it upsets you."

"No, I'm fine now," Neil said. "I was stupid. I'll have to tell Jane I'm sorry."

"She's sorry, too," said Emily. "She knows there'll never be another Sam."

Neil looked down at Sam, who was sitting beside his chair. He reached down and caressed the dog's head. Sam looked up at him, his eyes filled with love and trust.

"No," Neil said. "There never will."

When Bob's obedience class was over, the Parkers set off to Old Mill Farm. They walked across the fields; it was just the right gentle exercise for Sam. Neil kept him on the leash so he wouldn't be able to run and play. One of the problems, Mike Turner had said, would be to teach Sam that there were some things he couldn't do anymore.

At the farm, the Parkers went straight to the scullery door. Jane came out to meet them. As soon as she and Neil saw each other they both said, "I'm really sorry . . ." and burst out laughing. Jane bent down to pat Sam.

"I'm so glad he's getting better," she said.

"He won't ever be completely better," Neil said. He could accept that now. "But Mike says he'll probably live for years yet."

Sarah had already gone inside and was squealing happily over the puppies. The others followed her. Neil led Sam over to the whelping box where Delilah was proudly taking care of her pups. She was suckling them, and she bent her head around to give each of them an occasional lick. When Sam appeared she nosed him in a friendly way, but most of her attention was for the puppies.

"There, Sam," said Neil. "How does it feel to be a dad?"

Sam looked at his offspring with interest. Now that the puppies were properly clean and dry, they looked more like puppies: tiny black-and-white bodies, their eyes still closed, burrowing busily into their mother's flank.

"They're so sweet," said Emily.

"They're good ones," said Jane. "I bet Sam is a pedigree dog, you know. You can't hide quality."

Her praise warmed Neil's heart. Sam had shown

what a superb dog he was, in the competition and by fathering Delilah's pups.

"You'll have no trouble finding owners," said Bob. "You'll have a line all the way down the street."

"We'll keep at least one," Jane said. "Richard will need working dogs, and Border collies are the best. And I was thinking . . . Neil, I know you can't ever replace Sam. But if you want to change your mind, the offer's still open."

Neil was silent. The sight of the squirming bundle of puppies was doing something strange to his insides. He looked up at his parents.

"What do you think?"

Bob was grinning widely. Carole said, "If it's what you want."

"A male or a female?" Jane asked.

Neil took a deep breath. "A male, please," he said.

Jane bent over the litter. "There are two." She pointed them out to Neil. "OK, Delilah, no one's taking your pups away. We just want to look."

Neil looked at the two male pups. There wasn't a lot to choose between them. The smaller of the two was sucking vigorously, tucked close in to his mother's body, with a blissful look on his face. There was something about him that appealed to Neil. Maybe, even though he was so tiny, it was something of the energy that Neil loved in Sam. "That one," he said.

Jane lifted the puppy out of the nest and put him in Neil's hands. He felt soft and warm. Neil held him close and felt the tiny paws working.

"Oh, thank you," he said.

"What will you call him?" Sarah asked.

Neil's mind was a blank.

"What about a Bible name?" Jane suggested. "We've already got Sam and Delilah."

"Methuselah!" said Emily, giggling.

Neil made a face at her. "What about Jake?" he said. "Short for Jacob."

"I like that," said Bob.

"Jake," Neil repeated, trying out the feel of the

name. "Yes, that's good." He lifted the puppy so that he could look into his face. His eyes were still closed, his funny little nose scrunched up, his black-and-white coat sticking up in wisps. "Hi there, Jake," Neil said softly. "Come and meet your dad."